SYCAMORE

HAZEL

BIRCH

OAK

SCOTS PINE

T0022246

For L.I.
C.B.

For Mrs. Nock's class
C.V.

THE Things That I LOVE about TREES

Chris Butterworth

illustrated by Charlotte Voake

CANDLEWICK PRESS

It's spring!

And the thing
about trees that I love
in the spring is that
changes begin.

There are buds, like beads,
getting bigger
on the branches. . . .

Trees are plants (big ones!),
and spring is the time when most
plants put out new leaves.

6

The flower buds
on this plum tree
are opening into
blossoms, which are
buzzing with bees . . .

Bees visit the blossoms to collect nectar. Some pollen from each flower brushes on to a visiting bee, which carries it to the next flower.

and other buds
are opening into
brand-new leaves.

The trees are
waking up!

New leaves are usually
bright green and still a bit
crumpled. When you touch
them, they feel soft.

Birds and squirrels
build nests in the treetops,
safely hidden among
the new leaves.

In summer,
the thing about trees
that I love is how
big they look!

12

This one's as wide as our building.

Trees do most of their growing in spring
and early summer. Their roots suck up water
from under the earth. In hot weather, a big tree
can drink as much as a bathtubful every day!

Summer trees are shady
and so full of leaves that
when the wind blows,
they swish like the sea.

14

Leaves use sunshine
to make food that
the tree
needs
so that it
can
grow.

By summer, leaves are
thicker, stronger, and
darker green than
they were in spring.

The blossoms on the plum tree
have all dropped now,
but where each flower was,
a little green plum
is growing.

A plum flower can't
make its fruit
without the pollen
that the
bees carried.

A new plum needs to swell
and ripen for several weeks
in the summer sun before
it's juicy and good to eat.

In the fall, the days are
shorter and cooler, so leaves start
to change color and
begin to die.

The thing that I love
about trees in
the fall is how lots
of them change color:
from all shades of yellow
to pumpkin orange
and fire-engine red.

As well as bright leaves,
I see tree seeds and ripe fruit:
nuts for the squirrels,
berries for the mice,
and a sweet sticky plum
for a bird.

In the middle
of each plum is a seed
that can grow into
a new plum tree.

21

When a storm blows in,
the trees rain leaves!
(Catch one in the air,
and you can make
a wish.)

Some leaves that look
tiny high up on a tree
turn out to be big
on the ground.

Not all trees lose their leaves
in the fall. The ones that do
are called deciduous trees.
Trees that keep their leaves
are called evergreen.

23

In winter,
the thing that I love
about trees is how
bare they are.
You can lean
on the trunk
and look all
the way up to
the top.

(When you touch the bark,
it feels hard and rough.)

Trees that lose
their leaves
take a rest from
growing through
the dark,
chilly days
of winter.

Tree bark protects a tree from insects
and other animals that might eat it,
and also from too much heat or cold.

And when a storm comes,
thrashing the branches,
snapping off twigs,
and rocking the trunk,
the tree's roots hold
it safe in the ground

while it waits . . .

for the warm days of spring,
when the trees will begin
to wake up
all over again!

There are lots of games you can play and all kinds of things you can do with trees!

Build a hideout from big sticks and fallen branches.

Start a collection of pinecones, leaves, twigs, acorns, or chestnuts.

Use a fallen tree as a giant climbing frame.

Make pictures and shapes with fallen leaves and sticks.

Hide away in an old hollow trunk or under low-hanging leaves.

Turn over old logs and pieces of bark to go on a bug hunt. (A magnifying glass might come in handy.)

Stay very still and quiet to see the wild creatures that make their homes in the trees.

Index

Look up the pages to find out all about these tree things. Don't forget to look at both kinds of words —

this kind

and

this kind.

bark . . . 24–25

blossoms . . . 8–9, 16

branches . . . 6, 26

buds . . . 6, 8, 10

fruit . . . 9, 16–17, 21

growing . . . 13, 25

leaves . . . 6, 10–11, 14–15, 18–19, 21, 22–23, 25

pollen . . . 9, 16

roots . . . 13, 26

seeds . . . 21

sunshine . . . 15

trunk . . . 24, 26

A Plum-Tree Note

There are lots of different varieties of plum trees. They blossom and bear fruit at different times, depending on what kind they are and what climate they grow in. The one in this book is based on the Stanley plum tree.

SWEET CHESTNUT

BEECH